What if Dad gets lost at the zoo?

Ginette Lamont Clarke
and Florence Stevens

Illustrations by
Isabelle Langevin

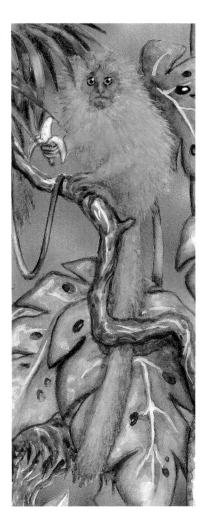

Tundra Books

Paul and Carol are playing with some toy animals while their father reads to them: "Zebras run across the grasslands of Africa. Lions watch from a rocky ledge. . ."

"Can zebras run faster than kangaroos?" asks Carol.

"Kangaroos don't run. They hop," Paul says. "And they don't live in the same place as zebras and lions."

Carol asks, "Don't all the animals ever live together?"

"Only in the zoo," their father answers. "You've never been to a zoo, have you?"

Carol and Paul are very excited. "Can we go right now? Today?"

"Maybe. I'll phone and see how late the zoo is open," their father answers. "You two go outside and play."

Carol says softly, "A zoo must be very big. . ."

"What will we do if Dad gets lost there?" asks Paul.

"If Dad gets lost at the zoo, I know what we could do," Carol says. "We could ask a parrot to help us. Parrots can talk."

"Parrots can't talk like people," Paul says. "They just repeat what they hear."

"We could teach a parrot to say, 'DADDY, DADDY, WHERE ARE YOU?'" suggests Carol.

"Anyway," Paul says, "Dad wouldn't get lost at the zoo. He'd be sitting on a bench reading his newspaper. All we need to do is look for a bench." He shakes his head. "He wouldn't get lost at the zoo, but I know where he could get lost."

"Where?" asks Carol.

"In a JUNGLE!"

"How could Dad get lost in a jungle?" asks Carol.

"Anyone can get lost in the jungle," Paul answers. "The trees are very tall and the leaves are bigger than umbrellas! It's so dark you can't even see the sky. And snakes crawl around and monkeys scream. Water drips all over you. . ."

"Stop," Carol yells. "Why would Dad get lost in the jungle? What would he be doing in a jungle anyway?"

"Catching butterflies!" says Paul, laughing.

"Then all we have to do is look for his butterfly net," Carol says. "But I know a worse place where he could get lost."

"Where?" asks Paul.

"With the ELEPHANTS!"

"What kind of elephants?" Paul asks. "Elephants with big ears or small ears?"

"Big elephants with small ears," Carol replies. "The ones that work in the forests of India. They are so strong they can pull trees right out of the ground and carry them away. And if Dad got lost there, the elephants make so much noise, he couldn't even ask the way because nobody would hear him."

"What would Dad be doing with elephants anyway?" asks Paul.

"Getting a ride!" answers Carol, smiling.

"Then all we'd have to do is look for an elephant with a little umbrella on its back and Dad would be in the seat," Paul says. "But I know a very strange place where he could get lost."

"Where?" asks Carol.

"In the DESERT!"

"What kind of desert?" wonders Carol.

"A big desert with lots of sand as far as you can see. And it's so hot you get thirsty, but there's no water to drink anywhere. And you think you see trees, but when you get to them, they aren't there at all. You go looking for the pyramids with camels and kangaroos. . ." explains Paul.

"There aren't any kangaroos around the pyramids," Carol says. "And what would Dad be doing there anyway?"

"Painting the desert!" replies Paul.

"Then all we'd have to do is look for his easel and we'd find him," Carol says. "But I know a terrible place where he could get lost."

"Where?" asks Paul.

"In a SWAMP!"

"What kind of swamp?" Paul asks.

Carol answers, "A swamp full of big green alligators and big brown crocodiles that swim fast. They have big mouths that open very wide and close with a snap! And trees stick out and catch you and hold you until the alligators and crocodiles come and. . ."

"Alligators and crocodiles don't live in the same swamp," Paul says. "And what would Dad be doing in a swamp anyway?"

"Fishing!" Carol laughs.

"Then all we'd have to do is look for his fishing boat and we'd find him," Paul says. "But I know a scarier place where he could get lost."

"Where?" asks Carol.

"In the GRASSLANDS!"

"What grasslands?" Carol asks.

"The grasslands of Africa," Paul answers. "The lion is the king of the beasts. When he roars, everybody is scared. He sits on a hill waiting for zebras to come by so that he can jump on them and eat them up. . ."

"Daddy lions don't hunt," Carol says. "They're lazy. All they do is sleep and show off. The mommy lion does the hunting. And after she has done all the work, the daddy lion wakes up and comes to eat. And what would Dad be doing in the grasslands anyway?"

"Taking pictures!" says Paul.

"Then all we'd have to do is look for his camera," Carol says. "But I know the worst place where he could get lost."

"Where?" asks Paul

"At the NORTH POLE!"

"The North Pole?" Paul asks. "How would Dad get lost there?"

"When there's a snowstorm you can't see anything," replies Carol. "It's cold, and you have to be careful because there are big white polar bears and they're hungry because all they have to eat are little penguins. . ."

"Penguins don't live at the North Pole." Paul says. "They live at the South Pole where there are no bears. And if Dad did get lost in a snowstorm, he'd build an igloo and stay in it until the storm went away. He wouldn't really be lost."

Carol nods her head. "Dad would never get lost anywhere. We're the ones who would get lost. What if we got lost in the dark with tigers all around us? What would we do?"

"Tigers?" asks Paul.

"Yes," Carol answers. "At night. They'd be hiding in the tall grass. All we would see are their eyes gleaming, watching us."

"There would only be one tiger." Paul says. "Tigers don't hunt together."

"One would be scary enough!" answers Carol.

"We could build a fire," Paul says. "Animals are afraid of fire."

"And we could yell," Carol agrees. "We could yell 'DADDY, DADDY!' " She starts to yell and Paul joins her.

Together they shout, "DADDY, DADDY, WHERE ARE YOU?"

"Here I am. What's wrong?" their father asks, running out of the house. "Are you ready to go to the zoo?"

"Look, Dad. We made a zoo in the sandbox," says Carol.

"It's not a zoo, it's a jungle," says Paul.

"It's a desert."

"No, it's the North Pole. . ."

"And we got lost!" The children laugh and so does their father.

"Come on. Let's go to the real zoo," their father says.

Paul and Carol arrive at the zoo with their father. He pays for the tickets, and they go through the gate and stop before a large map.

"What do you want to see first?" their father asks. "There are monkeys, crocodiles, camels, zebras, elephants, polar bears, lions, and even tigers."

"Is there a parrot in this zoo?" asks Carol.

"I'm sure there is," replies their father.

"We want to see it first," says Paul.

"First," their father says, "we'll buy some cotton candy, and then we'll go over and see the parrot."

©1991, Isabelle Langevin, illustrations
©1991, Ginette Lamont Clarke, Florence Stevens, text

Published in Canada by Tundra Books, Montreal, Quebec
H3G 1R4.

Published in the United States by Tundra Books of Northern
New York, Plattsburgh, N.Y. 12901

Library of Congress Catalog Number: 91-65365

Design by Michael Dias

Printed in Hong Kong by South China Printing Co. Ltd.

Canadian Cataloging in Publication Data

Stevens, Florence, 1928-
    What if Dad gets lost at the zoo?

ISBN 0-88776-265-4 (hardcover)
ISBN 0-88776-272-7(paperback)

(Issued also in French under title: Et si papa se perd au zoo?
ISBN 0-88776-266-2 (hc), ISBN 0-88776-273-5 (pb))

    1. French language — Readers (Primary). 2. French language
— Readers — 1950- . I. Stevens, Florence, 1928- . II. Langevin,
Isabelle. III. Title.

PE1119.C58932 1991   428.6   C91-090244-5

The publisher has applied funds from its Canada Council block
grant for 1991 toward the editing and production of this book.